SEAS AND OCEANS
FACTS & LISTS

SEAS AND OCEANS
FACTS & LISTS

Phillip Clarke

Designed by
Karen Tomlins and Luke Sargent

Digital imagery by Keith Furnival

Consultants: Dr Ben Wigham,
Southampton Oceanography Centre
and H.M. Hignett

Managing designer: Ruth Russell
Series editor: Judy Tatchell

02258

Internet Links

Throughout this book, we have suggested interesting Web sites where you can find out more about the oceans. To visit the sites, go to the **Usborne Quicklinks Web site** at **www.usborne-quicklinks.com** and type the keywords "ocean facts". There you will find links to click on to take you to all the sites. Here are some of the things you can do on the Web sites:

• See an undersea world through a live Webcam.

• Hunt for giant squid in the deep sea in an interactive animation.

• Take a virtual tour of a huge cargo ship.

Site availability

The links in **Usborne Quicklinks** are regularly reviewed and updated, but occasionally you may get a message that a site is unavailable. This might be temporary, so try again later, or even the next day. If any of the sites close down, we will, if possible, replace them with suitable alternatives, so you will always find an up-to-date list of sites in **Usborne Quicklinks**.

Internet safety

When using the Internet, please make sure you follow these guidelines:

• Ask your parent's or guardian's permission before you connect to the Internet.

• If you write a message in a Web site guest book or on a Web site message board, do not include any personal information such as your full name, address or telephone number, and ask an adult before you give your e-mail address.

• If a Web site asks you to log in or register by typing your name or e-mail address, ask permission from an adult first.

• If you do receive an e-mail from someone you don't know, tell an adult and do not reply to the e-mail.

• Never arrange to meet anyone you have talked to on the Internet.

Note for parents and guardians

The Web sites described in this book are regularly reviewed and the links in **Usborne Quicklinks** are updated. However, the content of a Web site may change at any time and Usborne Publishing is not responsible for the content on any Web site other than its own.

We recommend that children are supervised while on the Internet, that they do not use Internet Chat Rooms, and that you use Internet filtering software to block unsuitable material. Please ensure that your children read and follow the safety guidelines printed on the left. For more information, see the **Net Help** area on the **Usborne Quicklinks** Web site.

Computer not essential

If you don't have access to the Internet, don't worry. This book is a complete, superb, self-contained reference book on its own.

Contents

Salty Seas

Over two-thirds of the Earth is covered in water. Together, the Pacific, Atlantic, Indian, Southern and Arctic Oceans form a continuous stretch of water that covers an area nine times that of the Moon's surface.

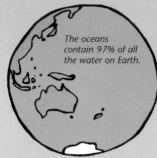

The oceans contain 97% of all the water on Earth.

The five oceans

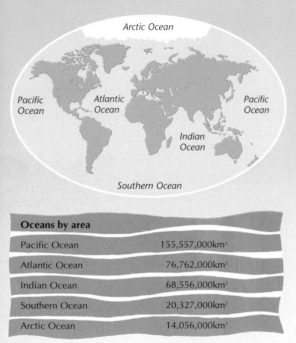

Arctic Ocean

Pacific Ocean

Atlantic Ocean

Pacific Ocean

Indian Ocean

Southern Ocean

Why is the sea blue?

On sunny days, sea water looks blue because it reflects blue light rays from the Sun. The Yellow Sea, near China, gets its name from yellow clay washed down by rivers. The Black Sea, near Russia, is coloured by black mud.

The White Sea, north of Russia, is so called because it is covered in ice for 200 days a year.

Oceans by area	
Pacific Ocean	155,557,000km²
Atlantic Ocean	76,762,000km²
Indian Ocean	68,556,000km²
Southern Ocean	20,327,000km²
Arctic Ocean	14,056,000km²

Ocean birth

Soon after the Earth was formed, 4,600 million years ago, the ocean began to take shape. Water vapour rose from the Earth's hot surface. As it cooled, it formed storm clouds, and the first rain fell, creating the first, boiling ocean.

Storms raged for thousands of years to form the first ocean.

There is enough salt in the oceans to cover the land with a layer 150m deep. Some of this salt comes from underwater volcanoes, but most is from the land. Rain dissolves salt in the rocks; rivers carry it to the sea.

Largest seas	Area
Weddell Sea (Southern Ocean)	8,000,000km²
Arabian Sea (Indian Ocean)	7,456,000km²
South China Sea (Pacific Ocean)	2,974,000km²
Mediterranean Sea (Atlantic Ocean)	2,505,000km²
Barents Sea (Arctic Ocean)	1,300,000km²

INTERNET LINKS

For links to Web sites where you can find an interactive map of the world's seas and oceans, an animation of the water cycle, or listen to undersea sounds, go to **www.usborne-quicklinks.com**

Ocean or sea?

A sea is an area within an ocean. Some seas are part of the open ocean, such as the Sargasso Sea in the Atlantic. Others, such as the South China Sea, are partly landlocked.

Sea plants first grew 3,500 million years ago. They were blue-green algae (also called cyanobacteria), and they gave off oxygen as they made their food. Algae still make over half of Earth's oxygen.

Blue-green algae are often in long chains stuck together with jelly.

China

Philippines

The South China Sea is shown in darker blue.

Dolphins live in most of the world's oceans. They can swim at speeds of up to 40kph.

Speedy sound

Sound travels more than four times faster through sea water than through air. It took just 144 minutes for the sound of an undersea explosion off Australia to reach Bermuda, halfway round the world.

Everlasting water

There is no new water on Earth. The same water moves from the oceans to the sky to the land. Rivers return the water to the oceans, and the cycle goes on.

Water just goes round and round.

Restless Oceans

The Earth's hard crust is in seven large pieces, and many smaller ones, called plates. These lie like giant rafts on the softer rock layer beneath. As plates collide or drift apart, they alter the oceans' shape and size.

Sliding under

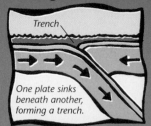

One plate sinks beneath another, forming a trench.

Where undersea plates collide, one plate is often pushed under another and melts back into the Earth. These areas, called subduction zones, form long, narrow trenches in the seabed, over 10km deep.

The Earth's plates fit together like pieces in a jigsaw puzzle.

The Himalayas were once part of the sea floor. Today, they are 500km from the sea. They formed 40 million years ago, when India drifted north and crashed into Asia, pushing seabed rocks 8km into the air.

Fossil seashells like this have been found on Mount Everest.

Ancient oceans

About 170 million years ago, all the continents formed one landmass, called Pangaea. Around it lay a vast ocean called Panthalassa.

As Pangaea split into continents, the Indian, Atlantic and Southern Oceans were formed. Panthalassa became the Pacific Ocean.

Part of Panthalassa jutted into the mainland of Pangaea, forming the Tethys Sea.

The movement of the Earth's plates began to form the oceans we know today.

Salt lake

About six million years ago, plates colliding together caused the Mediterranean Sea to become cut off from the oceans:

The Mediterranean Sea was cut off from the oceans as Morocco and Spain collided.

In about 1,000 years the water dried up, leaving the sea bottom caked in a layer of salt 1km thick.

Then the Atlantic Ocean rose. Over 100 years, water flowed back to the sea, in the biggest waterfall ever.

Island birth

In November 1963, an underwater volcano erupted near Iceland and formed a new island called Surtsey. Four days later, Surtsey was 61m long. Within 18 months the first leafy green plant was growing on the island.

When the eruption that created Surtsey began, it was thought to be a ship on fire.

Magma poured from the volcano, and cooled in the water, forming new rock.

Seaquakes

There are about a million earthquakes a year. Many happen underwater around the Pacific Ocean. The deepest seaquakes occur beneath ocean trenches, up to 750km below sea level. Most are never felt.

In the last Ice Age, 18,000 years ago, it was possible to walk from England to France. The sea level was over 120m lower than it is today. Since then, sea level has risen by about 8cm every 100 years.

INTERNET LINKS
To find links to Web sites about how the oceans were formed, go to **www.usborne-quicklinks.com**

Icebergs are formed when chunks break off the Antarctic ice sheet.

Seafloor spread

New seafloor crust is always being made. As undersea plates separate, liquid rock, known as magma, rises to fill the gap and solidifies into mountains. The ocean floor grows about 4cm wider every year.

Flood warning

Today, ice covers about a tenth of the Earth. A temperature rise of 4°C could melt all the ice and raise sea level by about 70m. Coastal cities, such as Sydney, Tokyo and New York, would be drowned.

Under the Sea

Seascape

Under the sea, the landscape is as varied as on land. Parts of this seascape have different names, according to their depth below sea level.

Land

Continental shelf
(less than 200m deep)

Continental margin

Continental slope
(less than 2.5km deep)

Continental rise (less than 4km deep)

Abyssal plain (over 4km deep)

On the shelf

The continental shelf varies in how far it extends from the shore: from 1km on South America's Pacific coast to 1,200km around northern Siberia. Most fish are caught over continental shelves.

Great white sharks hunt fish and other animals over continental shelves.

Deep peaks

There are underwater mountains, known as seamounts, in all oceans. Great Meteor Seamount in the Atlantic is over 100km wide at its base and 4km high.

Mount Everest

Great Meteor Seamount

INTERNET LINKS
For links to Web sites about the undersea landscape, go to
www.usborne-quicklinks.com

Rolling plains

The flattest places on Earth are the stretches of deep seabed called abyssal plains. They cover nearly half the sea floor. You could walk on them around the globe without climbing any more than 2m.

The tallest mountain on Earth is not Mount Everest, but Mauna Kea in the Pacific Ocean. This volcano rises 10,203m from the sea floor to form one of the Hawaiian islands. Everest is over 1,000m lower.

Everest

Sea level

Mauna Kea

Under pressure

The deeper you go under the sea, the greater the pressure of water pushing down on you. In the deepest ocean, the pressure on you would be equivalent to the weight of an elephant balanced on a stamp.

Earth's deepest point is the 11,022m deep Mariana Trench in the Pacific. If a 1kg weight fell into the trench, it would take over an hour to reach the bottom.

This is a submersible. It can withstand huge pressures to take explorers safely into the deep ocean.

Ocean	Average depth	Deepest point
Pacific Ocean	4,200m	11,022m
Atlantic Ocean	3,300m	9,560m
Indian Ocean	3,900m	9,000m
Southern Ocean	3,730m	8,264m
Arctic Ocean	1,300m	5,450m

Avalanche

Seaquakes* can trigger avalanches of mud and sand which cascade down the continental slope. They can cover areas of the seabed the size of France with a layer of mud over 1m thick.

Deep sea carpet

About three quarters of the deep ocean floor is covered in a smooth ooze, mostly around 300m thick. It is made up of the dead bodies of animals and plants which drifted down and mixed with mud. The ooze layer grows just 6m every million years.

The remains of tiny shelled sea creatures, like these, sink slowly to the ocean floor.

Cold and dark

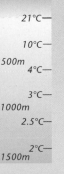

21°C—	
10°C—	
500m	
4°C—	
3°C—	
1000m	
2.5°C—	
2°C—	
1500m	

The sea gets darker and colder the deeper you go. Most sunlight is absorbed in the top 10m of water. No light at all reaches below 1,000m, even on the sunniest day.

Oceans in Motion

The wind drives huge bands of water, called currents, around the world. The Antarctic circumpolar current flows around Antarctica. It carries over 2,000 times more water than Earth's largest river, the Amazon.

The world's main currents

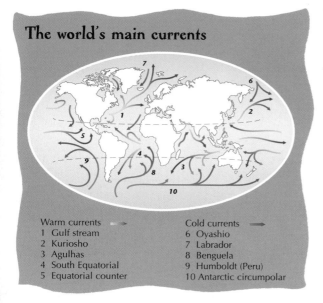

Warm currents
1 Gulf stream
2 Kuriosho
3 Agulhas
4 South Equatorial
5 Equatorial counter

Cold currents
6 Oyashio
7 Labrador
8 Benguela
9 Humboldt (Peru)
10 Antarctic circumpolar

Welling up

Near Peru, the cold Humboldt current raises minerals from the deep, feeding tiny sea plants. These in turn are food for millions of fish. In one year, 10 million tonnes of anchovies may be caught.

A school of anchovies

12

The ground under our feet rises and falls twice a day, just like the ocean tides. When the Moon is directly overhead, it rises by half a metre.

Timely tides

Twice a day, tides make the sea level rise and fall. Tides are caused by the Moon and Sun's gravity pulling water into giant bulges on the Earth.

Spring tide

→ *Moon's orbit*
→ *Pull of Moon and Sun*

When the Moon and Sun pull in a straight line, they cause very high and very low tides. These are called spring tides.

Neap tide

→ *Moon's orbit*
→ *Pull of Moon*

When the Moon and Sun pull at right angles, the tides are more even. These are "neap tides". Spring and neap tides occur twice monthly.

Extreme tides

The greatest tides occur in the Bay of Fundy, Canada. They can rise high enough to cover a 5 storey building.

Tsunami terrors

Tsunamis are giant waves caused by earthquakes or undersea eruptions. They move as fast as jet planes. As they near land they rear up to great heights and can drown whole islands.

Undersea eruptions shake the seabed, causing the sea to form long, low tsunami waves.

If tsunamis reach the coast, they are squeezed up into huge waves that can cause disaster.

Making waves

Waves are caused by wind blowing over the sea. The stronger the wind and the longer it blows, the bigger the waves. Waves only break the water's surface.

Submarines only need to dive 100m to avoid even the harshest storms.

Junk that washes up on beaches is used to study how winds and currents work. In 1992, a ship spilled a cargo of rubber ducks in the Pacific. Scientists tracked their progress. Many were found in Alaska, but others are still going!

INTERNET LINKS
To find links to Web sites about waves and ocean currents, go to
www.usborne-quicklinks.com

Giant waves

The highest recorded natural wave was seen in the Pacific Ocean in 1933. It measured 34m – the height of a 10 storey building.

A wave is energy from the wind moving through water.

Along the Shore

Coast to coast

The combined length of all coastlines would reach to the Moon and halfway back. These are the top ten coastlines:

Country	Length
Canada	93,711km
Indonesia	54,716km
Greenland	44,087km
Russia	37,653km
Philippines	36,289km
Australia	25,760km
USA	19,924km
New Zealand	15,134km
China	14,500km
Greece	13,676km

Prickly character

Most sea urchins are fist-sized, but some grow to 36cm across. Using their spines and sharp teeth, sea urchins burrow into sand and rock. Over 20 years, one Californian sea urchin drilled 1cm into a solid steel girder.

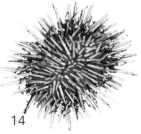

Slimy seaweed

A danger faced by life on the shore is drying up when the tide goes out. Seaweeds keep moist by covering themselves with slimy mucus. The world's longest seaweed is the Pacific giant kelp. It grows over 50m long.

Giant kelp grows very quickly: up to 60cm a day.

Taking a beating

The coastline is constantly being worn away by the waves. This is called erosion. The waves carve out cliffs, caves and arches along the shore.

This rock arch off the coast of Oregon, USA, was carved out by the sea.

Purple sea urchins — very prickly

The highest sea cliffs in the world are on the north coast of Molokai, Hawaii. They are over a kilometre high.

The sea cliffs of Molokai are over three times as tall as the Eiffel Tower in France.

Sticky customer

Animals living on the shoreline have to survive being battered by the waves. A limpet clings to its rocky perch so firmly that it would take a force 2,000 times its own weight to prise it off.

Limpets live on algae, which they scrape from the rocks with a rasping tongue.

Mangroves

Mangrove trees grow in huge swamps where tropical rivers flow into the sea. The trees may be 40m tall. Salt water can kill plants so mangroves eject waste salt through their leaves or store it in old leaves which they then shed.

The mangroves' long, tangled roots anchor them in the mud.

Mudskippers are odd fish that spend much of their time out of the water in mangrove swamps. They breathe through their skin.

Mudskippers flip themselves along with their tails. They can leap over half a metre.

Hitching a lift

Hermit crabs borrow discarded seashells to house their soft bodies. As they grow, they find a bigger shell to live in.

A hermit crab in a borrowed shell

Seashore molluscs

Molluscs are a huge group of animals found on land and in water. They range from squid and octopuses to tiny seashells. These are some of the molluscs found along the shore:

Bivalves (Double shell)	Univalves (Single shell)
Mussel	Limpet
Oyster	Winkle
Scallop	Whelk
Razor shell	Cowrie

Sand colours

Sand forms when wind and rain wear down rocks into tiny pieces. Yellow sand contains tiny pieces of quartz. Pink or white sand contains coral, and black sand contains volcanic rock or coal. Rare green sand contains the mineral olivine.

Coral Reefs

Coral reefs are built by tiny animals called polyps. They use minerals in sea water to build skeletons around themselves. Polyps live in vast colonies. After death, they leave layers of hard limestone skeleton.

Most reef-building coral is very sensitive. It grows best in water with these features:

1. Temperature	Warm: 25-29°C	
2. Depth	Less than 25m deep	
3. Saltiness	No saltier than 30-40 parts per thousand	
4. Purity	Must be clear and unpolluted	

Every day, coral grows a new skeleton layer. The way it grows is affected by the seasons. Scientists studying fossil coral think that 400 million years ago a year was 400 days long. Days have shortened by three quarters of a second every century.

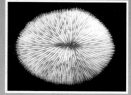

Skeleton of the mushroom coral

Coral islands

The Pacific has thousands of coral islands, called atolls. Thousands of years ago, they were coral reefs around volcanic islands. The volcano sank, but the coral kept growing to form a low-lying atoll around a shallow lagoon.

30 million BC
Volcano fringed with coral

Today
Coral atoll with lagoon

Some like it cold

Some of the world's largest coral reefs are actually found in the deep, cold waters of the North Atlantic. Off Scotland are hundreds of odd, coral-covered mounds called the Darwin Mounds. They are home to giant one-celled animals called xenophyophores, which can be over 20cm wide.

Coral reefs are home to thousands of animal species.

Home, sweet home

Pencil-thin pearlfish live in the bodies of sea cucumbers. Up to three spend the day sleeping inside one sea cucumber, their heads sticking out of its tail end.

A pearlfish wriggling, tail first, into the body of a sea cucumber

Clamming up

The giant clam has the largest shell in the world. It can be 1.2m wide, and weigh over a quarter of a tonne. The two halves of the shell fit together so tightly that they can grip a thin wire.

Good shot

Pistol shrimps are just 5cm long but have deadly weapons. When hunting fish, the shrimp snaps its large right claw, making a sound like a pistol shot. This sends shockwaves through the water, stunning the fish. The shrimp then has time to close in for the kill.

Small cleaner wrasse run beauty parlours on the reef. Larger fish queue to have dead skin and parasites picked off their bodies. Even fierce moray eels sit still as their teeth are cleaned.

Cleaner wrasse at work

Longest reef

The longest coral reef is the Great Barrier Reef. It stretches over 2,000km off the coast of Queensland, Australia. It is the biggest structure ever formed by a living thing – it can even be seen from the Moon.

The Great Barrier Reef is shown in pink below.

Australia

Thorny problem

The Great Barrier Reef is being eaten away by crown of thorns starfish. To digest the coral, they push their stomachs out of their bodies to cover it. 15 starfish can eat an area of reef as big as a soccer pitch in 2½ years.

Crown of thorns starfish

INTERNET LINKS
To find links to Web sites about coral reefs, and the animals that live in them, go to **www.usborne-quicklinks.com**

Giant clam

Small Fry

Billions of tiny plants, called phytoplankton (meaning "drifting plants"), float near the sea surface. They use sunlight, and minerals from the water, to make their own food.

Without phytoplankton, little could live in the sea. They are eaten by small sea animals (zooplankton) which in turn are eaten by fish. Over two million million tonnes of phytoplankton grow each year.

Large sea predators

Fish

Zooplankton

Phytoplankton

Phytoplankton form the basis of the ocean food supply.

The world's tiniest crabs have shells less than 6.5mm long. They are called pea crabs. They live and feed inside the shells of oysters, scallops and mussels.

Pea crab in a mussel shell

Titchy tiddlers

The smallest known sea fish is the dwarf goby from the Indian Ocean. Adults are only about 9mm long and could easily fit on a fingernail. Another dwarf goby, from Samoa, is the world's lightest fish. It would take 500 of them to weigh just 1g.

Part-time plankton

Sea slugs start life as tiny zooplankton with shells, floating near the sea surface. They grow up without having to compete with adults for food and space. Later they turn into adults without shells, such as the one below.

This extraordinary creature is an adult sea slug. This type grows 25mm long.

Short shark

The world's smallest shark is the spined pygmy shark from the Pacific Ocean. Adults measure just 15cm long. This is 120 times shorter than the whale shark, the world's largest shark.

Spined pygmy shark (a quarter life size)

! The main diet of the huge blue whale is a tiny, shrimp-like animal called krill. Krill are just 6cm long, but live in vast shoals. A blue whale sieves four tonnes of krill from the sea daily.

Shoals of krill can be several kilometres in length.

Blowing bubbles

The janthina snail lives at the sea surface. To stay afloat it blows bubbles, joining them together to make a raft from which it hangs upside down.

Red alert

In spring, many types of phytoplankton breed quickly in the warm weather. If those called dinoflagellates are involved, this can cause disaster. They are very poisonous. They turn the sea blood-red, with as many as 6,000 of them in one drop of water. They kill millions of fish and shellfish.

Dinoflagellates – tiny but deadly

INTERNET LINKS
To find links to Web sites about small sea creatures, go to
www.usborne-quicklinks.com

Seahorse slowcoach

Seahorses are the slowest fish. They hover in the water, powered by their tiny back fins. Even at top speed, it would take a seahorse 2½ days to travel 1km. Dwarf seahorses live in the Gulf Stream current, south of Bermuda. They are just 40mm long.

Dwarf seahorse (three times life size)

Smallest fry	Group	Average size
Ammonicera rota	Shells	0.5mm long
Sea biscuit	Sea urchin	5.5mm wide
Cushion star	Starfish	9mm wide
Parateuthis tunicata	Squid	12.7mm long
Octopus arborescens	Octopus	50mm wide
Cape lobster	Lobster	10cm long
Kemps ridley	Turtle	70cm long

Life in the Depths

Deep in the oceans, the water is pitch black and very cold. Despite this, thousands of fish and invertebrates live there.

Lantern fish light up the deep.

| Sunlit zone | Sargassum weed | Jellyfish | Mackerel |

200m

Flashlight fish

Lantern fish

Twilight zone

Viperfish

Giant isopod

Black dragonfish

1,000m

Hagfish

Deep-sea angler fish

Midnight zone
(Bathyal zone)

Vampire squid

Bristlemouth

Flashlight fish

Many deep-sea fish make their own lights. Flashlight fish have patches under their eyes which contain billions of glowing bacteria. If danger comes, they hide the lights with flaps of skin.

Flashlight fish with glowing eye patches

Many deep-sea prawns are bright red. Red is hard to see in deep water, and many deep-sea fish are colour-blind. One fish, the black dragonfish, has eyes that can see it. It also shines its own red light to hunt for the prawns.

Sticking together

Finding a mate is hard in the dark, so angler fish make sure they stay in touch. The male weighs half a million times less than the female. He grips her with his teeth and their bodies merge. All that is left of him is a pouch on her side which fertilizes her eggs.

Angling for food

An angler fish uses lights to trap food. A long, thin fin like a fishing rod grows over its head. It has a glowing bulb dangling on the end, which acts like bait. Small fish mistake it for a meal and swim straight into the angler's mouth.

The angler fish's lure is made up of tiny, glowing bacteria.

INTERNET LINKS
To find links to Web sites about the creatures of the deep go to
www.usborne-quicklinks.com

If attacked, the eel-like hagfish wraps itself in a cocoon of sticky slime. To leave the cocoon, it ties itself in a knot, then passes the knot down its body, wiping the slime away.

A hagfish getting knotted

Vicious viper

The viperfish is named for its long fangs and snake-like body. When hunting another sea animal, it swims rapidly forward, jaws open, and impales it on its front teeth. It also has lights inside its mouth which attract curious prey.

Viperfish have rows of hexagon-shaped lights along the sides of their bodies. These may be used to attract mates.

Roly-poly monsters

Giant isopods live 1km down on the sea floor. These armour-plated invertebrates are related to the common pill bug. When threatened, they roll up into a ball just like their land-dwelling relatives.

Giant isopods grow half a metre long.

Undersea lake

Scientists exploring 900m down in the Gulf of Mexico made an amazing discovery: a lake. Called a brine pool, its water is much saltier, and so heavier, than the sea water above. Its shores are surrounded by thousands of mussels which are able to make energy from methane gas seeping from the pool. This means they can live without sunlight.

These mussels live as near to the brine pool as they can – but if they fall in, they die.

The viperfish's teeth are so long that they do not all fit inside its mouth.

Animal	Greatest depth found
Prawn	6,373m
Sea urchin	7,340m
Sea spider	7,370m
Barnacle	7,880m
Fish (brotulid)	8,372m
Sponge	9,990m
Starfish	9,990m
Sea snail	10,687m
Sea anemone	10,730m
Sea cucumber	10,911m

Deeper Still

Over half the ocean floor lies below 4,000m, in the "abyssal zone". 6,000m down, trenches* plunge deeper still. This is the "hadal zone", named after Hades, the ancient Greek world of the dead; yet it is far from dead – millions of animals live there.

Tripod fish

Tripod fish have three very long fins. They use them like stilts to rest on the seafloor, while waiting for drifting food.

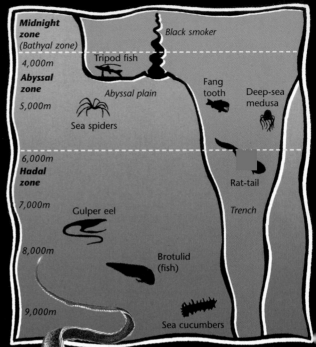

Midnight zone (Bathyal zone)

Black smoker

4,000m

Tripod fish

Abyssal zone

Fang tooth

Deep-sea medusa

Abyssal plain

5,000m

Sea spiders

6,000m

Hadal zone

Rat-tail

7,000m

Gulper eel

Trench

8,000m

Brotulid (fish)

9,000m

Sea cucumbers

Tripod fish resting on the sea floor

Sea cucumbers are found on the trench floors in herds of thousands. The most common trench animals by far, they eat mud, and filter out its nutrients.

Sea cucumber grazing

Big mouth

Gulper eels feed on dead animals drifting down from the surface. A tiny shrimp may take a week to fall 3km, so the eels make the most of any food they find. They have huge mouths and stretchy stomachs for swallowing prey larger than themselves.

Gulper eels swim onto their prey with their enormous mouths gaping wide.

*See *Sliding under*, page 8

Deep drummer

Rat-tails are one of the commonest deep-sea fish. Males are believed to attract mates in the dark depths by making a drumming noise with muscles inside their bodies.

Rat-tails can grow over a metre in length.

Deep sea problem	Adaptation	Example
Food is scarce	Grow more slowly Big mouth to catch food	Deep-sea clam Gulper eel
No light	Make own lights Developed sense of smell Super-developed eyes Movement-sensing organs	Lantern fish Angler fish Squid Brotulid (fish)

Black smokers

In some parts of the ocean where new seafloor is forming*, there are openings, called vents, which pour out super-hot water. Minerals from the rock build up around the vents into chimney stacks as tall as houses. Mineral-rich water gushes out of them.

Minerals in vent water turn it as dark as smoke.

Sea spiders

Sea spiders are distant cousins of land spiders. They stride around the sea floor on their long legs, feeding on anemones with their tube-like mouths.

Sea spiders are found in most seas.

INTERNET LINKS
To find links to Web sites about deep ocean vents, and the animals that live around them, go to **www.usborne-quicklinks.com**

A colony of giant tube worms

Some animals even live in deep Pacific vents, where the water is full of toxic chemicals and over 300°C. The strangest are giant tube worms that grow up to 2m long. Their bodies contain bacteria that make energy from the chemicals.

*See *Seafloor spread*, page 8

Attack and Defence

The great white shark has huge jaws filled with rows of triangular, razor-sharp teeth. Each tooth may be over 7cm long. As the front teeth wear out, the next row moves forward to replace them. Odd objects have been found in sharks' stomachs, including coats, a full bottle of wine and a porcupine.

Great white shark

Super smell

Sharks can smell blood from injured prey nearly 500m away. The nostrils of a hammerhead shark are at the ends of its hammer-shaped head. If it smells food, it swings its head from side to side to find the way to it.

The hammerhead shark – named for obvious reasons

Electric shock

Some fish use electric shocks to kill prey and defend themselves. The most powerful electric sea fish is the black torpedo ray. It makes enough electricity to power a television set.

Black torpedo ray

Deadly tentacles

The Portuguese man-of-war stuns prey with its long, stinging tentacles. These trail over 30m from its floating body. Once they have trapped some food, the tentacles can shrink quickly to 15cm long, so that it can be passed to the mouth.

Portuguese man-of-war

A starfish can escape its attackers by leaving some arms behind. All starfish can grow new arms, but some can grow a whole new body from just a tiny piece of arm.

Starfish may look odd while they are regrowing limbs.

Sinister stones

Stonefish have double protection. They are well camouflaged on the sea floor, looking just like weed-covered rocks. They also have poisonous spines, which can pierce a diver's rubber shoe.

Can you spot the stonefish?

A sea cucumber has a striking way of foiling enemies. If one comes too close, it entangles it with sticky, spaghetti-like threads, enabling the cucumber to flee.

A sea cucumber fending off a crab

Poison platter

Parts of the death puffer fish are highly poisonous, and can kill a person in two hours. It is eaten in Japan, but chefs must train for three years before serving it. People still die from eating it.

Hired defences

Spanish shawl sea slugs combine self-defence with a good meal. They eat sea anemones, complete with their stinging cells. The cells travel through the slug's body and rest just under its skin. If the sea slug is touched, the borrowed stinging cells shoot into its enemy.

Spanish shawl sea slug

Sailing by

The sailfish can swim at 109kph – faster than the cheetah, the fastest land animal. At high speed, the fish's sail-like back fin folds down into a groove, and its other fins press close to its body.

Sailfish cruising...

Sailfish at full throttle

INTERNET LINKS
To find links to Web sites about ocean predators and prey, go to
www.usborne-quicklinks.com

Smokescreen

Cuttlefish squirt out thick clouds of brown ink to confuse their enemies. This gives the cuttlefish time to escape. Cuttlefish ink is called sepia, and was once used as artists' ink and in photography.

Cuttlefish can change colour to match their surroundings.

Fish	Top speed
Sailfish	109kph
Bluefin tuna	100kph
Swordfish	90kph
Marlin	80kph
Wahoo	77kph
Yellowfin tuna	74kph
Blue shark	69kph
Flying fish	56kph
Barracuda	43kph
Mackerel	33kph

Sea Mammals

Until about 65 million years ago, the ancestors of whales and dolphins lived on land. Here are some of the ways they later adapted to water:

Pakicetus, the earliest known whale, probably spent most of its time on land.

- Bodies became streamlined for swimming.
- Front legs became flippers.
- Back legs disappeared altogether.
- Nostrils became a blowhole on the top of the head.
- Hair was replaced by a thick, warm layer of fat, called blubber, under the skin.

Record breaking blues

The blue whale is the largest sea mammal, and the biggest animal ever. An adult can weigh up to 190 tonnes – as much as 50 rhinos. Its tongue alone weighs three tonnes, heavier than 35 men.

Mammal group	Members
Cetaceans	Whales; dolphins; porpoises
Pinnipeds	Seals; sealions; walruses
Sirenians	Manatees; dugongs

A newborn blue whale can weigh over five tonnes – a thousand times heavier than a newborn human. By the age of seven months, it weighs as much as two buses.

The biggest whale on record was 33m long.

A baby blue whale drinks 600 litres of its mother's milk a day.

Sperm whales can hold their breath for two hours. One was found with two deep-sea sharks in its stomach. It must have dived 3,000m to catch them.

Bubble trouble

A humpback whale can trap its food by blowing bubbles. It circles a shoal of fish and blows a big net of bubbles around them. This confuses and traps the fish. The whale then swims up, mouth open, gulping the fish down.

Humpback whale

Mammal	Diet	Daily amount
Blue whale	Krill, shrimps	4 tonnes
Sperm whale	Squid, sharks	1 tonne
Elephant seal	Squid, fish	200kg
Orca (killer whale)	Seals, birds, sharks	45kg
Bottlenose dolphin	Fish, eels, hermit crabs	8-15kg

Dolphin detective

Dolphins use sound to navigate underwater. They give out clicks much higher than humans can hear. If the sounds hit objects in the water, they send back echoes. From these, the dolphin can tell where and what an object is.

Dolphins use echoes to hunt for fish.

echo echo

click click

A walrus has about 700 whiskers on its snout. It uses them to find shellfish under the sea. The whiskers are so thick, Inuit people use them as toothpicks.

A walrus's whiskers are 40 times thicker than a cat's.

Actual size

Sea elephant

The biggest pinniped is the huge southern elephant seal. The largest on record was 6.5m long and weighed 4 tonnes. If it reared up, it would have towered up to 3m in height.

Southern elephant seals

Speedy seals

Seals, sealions and walruses belong to a group of sea mammals called pinnipeds. The fastest pinniped is the Californian sealion. It can speed through the water at 40kph. Leopard seals also swim quickly when hunting penguins. To land, they rocket out of the water and crash onto the ice.

INTERNET LINKS

To find links to Web sites about mammals that live in the sea, go to **www.usborne-quicklinks.com**

Californian sealions are amazing acrobats.

Mermaid myth

Some say that manatees started the mermaid legend. When Christopher Columbus first saw one, he wrote that mermaids were not as beautiful as he had heard.

Manatee.... or mermaid?

Ocean Giants

The whale shark is the world's biggest fish. It grows over 18m long and weighs 20 tonnes – as much as five rhinos. It also has the thickest skin of any animal: it is like tough rubber, 10cm thick. Despite its size, this huge fish eats only plankton.

Whale sharks suck in huge amounts of water, sieve out the plankton, then blow the water out through gill slits (openings for breathing)

The gill slits are in this area.

The Arctic lion's mane jellyfish has a mane of tentacles which can trail for over 36m – longer than a blue whale. It is the world's largest jellyfish.

King crab

Crabs, lobsters and shrimps belong to a group of animals called crustaceans. Japanese spider crabs are the largest crustaceans known. The biggest spider crab ever found measured 3.7m across its front claws.

Spider crabs are named for their long, spindly legs.

Arctic lion's mane jellyfish

Manta rays have special fins for feeding.

Mighty manta

Diamond-shaped manta rays are the largest type of ray. They can weigh over two tonnes and have an 8m "wingspan". Rays swim through the water by flapping their wings. They can also leap 2m out of the water.

INTERNET LINKS
To find links to Web sites about the giants that live in the ocean, go to **www.usborne-quicklinks.com**

Awesome oarfish

Sharks and rays have skeletons of gristly cartilage. Other fish have bony skeletons. The longest bony fish is the oarfish. It can grow over 15m in length: longer than a bus.

Prize pearl

Sometimes, clams and oysters get irritating parasites or sand grains in their shells. They coat them with layers of calcium carbonate, forming pearls. The biggest pearl, the 6.4kg Pearl of Lao-Tzu, came from a giant clam.

Natural pearls, like the one in this oyster, are very rare. Just one is found in every 10,000 shells.

Ocean giant	Group	Biggest ever
Giant Pacific octopus	Octopus	4m long
Pacific leatherback	Turtle	2.54m long
Midgardia xandaros	Starfish	1.38m wide
Loggerhead sponge	Sponge	1.05m tall
Trumpet conch	Snail	0.77m long
Discoma	Sea anemone	0.61m wide
Giant clam	Bivalve	333kg
American lobster	Lobster	20kg

Squids in

The giant squid is the largest known invertebrate. The biggest giant squid on record washed up in Thimble Tickle Bay, Canada, in 1878. It was 17m long and weighed over two tonnes. Huge as they are, scientists have never seen an adult alive in its natural surroundings.

The eyes of giant squid are the size of basketballs: the biggest of any animal.

Ocean sunfish start life as a tiny egg the size of a pinhead, yet an adult is the size of a small truck: over 3m long, and weighing over 2 tonnes. The ocean sunfish is the heaviest bony fish.

The favourite food of the ocean sunfish is the moon jellyfish.

Birds of the Sea

There are about 300 sea bird species. They are divided into three groups (see right), depending on where they find their food.

Coast birds
cormorant; pelican; gull

Offshore birds
diving petrel; penguin; puffin; frigate bird; tern; gannet; guillemot

Open ocean birds
albatross; fulmar; petrel; kittiwake; shearwater; skua

Frigate express

The magnificent frigate bird is the fastest sea bird. It can fly at over 150kph. On some South Sea islands, people have trained frigate birds to carry messages between islands.

About tern

Many sea birds travel far between their feeding and breeding grounds. Each year the Arctic tern flies from the Arctic to the Antarctic and back again, a round trip of over 40,000km. Arctic terns start to fly south when they are just two or three months old.

In its lifetime, an Arctic tern flies the same distance as a return trip to the Moon.

Salt surplus

Sea birds take in lots of salt water as they feed. Too much salt kills birds, so special glands in their heads remove salt from the water. It trickles out of the birds' nostrils.

Sea birds lose salt through their nostrils.

Skuas and gulls have built-in sunglasses. Their eyes contain drops of reddish oil, which block out the harsh sunlight and the glare reflected from the sea.

Head over heels

Sea eagles perform highly unusual courtship displays. The male dives down towards the female, and the two birds lock their talons together. They then plummet downwards, turning cartwheels in mid-air.

Sea wanderer

The wandering albatross has the longest wingspan of any living bird – up to 3.5m. It glides on air currents across the Southern Ocean. If the winds are right, an albatross can fly 1,000km in a day.

Albatrosses are very efficient gliders, conserving energy as they soar.

Guillemots live in colonies of over 14,000 birds. They lay their eggs on narrow cliff ledges. The eggs are long and have pointed ends: ideally adapted not to fall off. If they are knocked, they just roll in a circle.

Guillemot eggs roll around, but not away.

Baby sitting

Emperor penguins nest on the Antarctic ice in midwinter, enduring temperatures of –62°C. The female lays one egg, then swims off. The male stays to tend the egg. He balances it on his feet and spends about nine weeks without moving or eating. The female returns to feed the chick when it hatches.

INTERNET LINKS
To find links to Web sites about sea birds go to
www.usborne-quicklinks.com

Spitting with rage

To drive intruders away from their nests, fulmars spit at them. Fulmars eat plankton, which makes the spit oily and smelly. They can hit targets up to a metre away very accurately.

Fulmars live in and around cold seas.

Penguins have special flaps to keep eggs and chicks warm.

Walking on water

Wilson's storm petrel is one of the smallest sea birds. As it flutters above the sea looking for plankton to eat, it pats the water's surface with its feet. This makes it seem to be walking on the water.

Wilson's storm petrel is the most common sea bird.

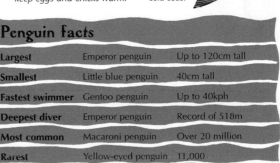

Penguin facts

Largest	Emperor penguin	Up to 120cm tall
Smallest	Little blue penguin	40cm tall
Fastest swimmer	Gentoo penguin	Up to 40kph
Deepest diver	Emperor penguin	Record of 518m
Most common	Macaroni penguin	Over 20 million
Rarest	Yellow-eyed penguin	11,000
Most northerly	Galápagos penguin	From Galápagos Islands

The Pacific Ocean

The Pacific is the largest ocean, covering about a third of the Earth. At its widest point, between Panama and Malaysia, it stretches nearly halfway round the world.

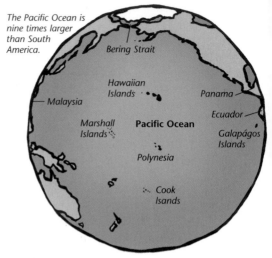

The Pacific Ocean is nine times larger than South America.

Bering Strait

Hawaiian Islands

Malaysia

Panama

Ecuador

Marshall Islands

Pacific Ocean

Galápagos Islands

Polynesia

Cook Isands

Vital statistics

Area	155,557,000km²
Widest point	17,700km
Narrowest point	11,000km
Average depth	4,200m
Greatest depth	11,022m

Land bridge

The Pacific's narrowest part is the Bering Strait, which divides the USA and Russia by 85km. 14,000 years ago, the sea level was lower, and the Strait was dry land. The first people to live in North America crossed over this land bridge.

Sea serpents

There are about 50 species of Pacific sea snake, ranging from 1-3m in length. All use poison to kill fish for food. One drop of sea snake venom could kill three people.

Sea snakes are the most poisonous of all snakes.

Epic voyages

Pacific island sailors were the first to explore the Pacific, over 2,000 years ago. They were experts at navigating by the wind, waves, Sun and stars.

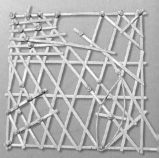

Marshall Islanders used stick charts, like this, to map currents around their islands (marked by shells).

Grey whales swim 20,000km each year. They spend the summer feeding in the Arctic. They then swim south along the Pacific coast to breed near Mexico, returning north in the spring.

Grey whales' bodies are often covered with barnacles.

Mountain maker

Along Chile's coast, the undersea plate that forms the Pacific floor meets the South American plate. This causes the continent to buckle upwards as the Pacific plate dives beneath it*. This process formed the Andes mountains about 80 million years ago, and they are still growing.

The Pacific floor sinks under the continent of South America.

South America buckles, and the Andes grow.

Sea dreams

Sea otters live on the Pacific coast of North America, in beds of giant kelp**. They spend most of their lives at sea, even sleeping in the water.

Sea otters wind strands of kelp around their bodies to stop them drifting away as they sleep.

Giant Galapágos tortoises can live for 200 years – longer than all other land animals. They live in the Galapágos Islands, west of Ecuador. These are also home to rare marine iguanas, the only lizards that live mainly in the sea.

Giant Galapágos tortoise

Tropical islands

The Pacific is dotted with islands. Over 100 ancient volcanoes make up the Hawaiian islands – a chain 2,800km long. Hawaii itself is made up of two huge volcanoes – Mauna Loa and Mauna Kea.

INTERNET LINKS
To find links to Web sites with more information on the Pacific Ocean, go to **www.usborne-quicklinks.com**

This beautiful lagoon is in the Cook Islands.

*See *Sliding under*, page 8; **See *Slimy seaweed*, page 14

The Atlantic Ocean

Vital statistics

Area	76,762,000km²
Widest part	4,830km
Narrowest part	2,848km
Average depth	3,300m
Greatest depth	9,560m

Still growing

The Atlantic is the second largest ocean, covering a fifth of the Earth. Each year, it grows about 4cm wider, pushing Europe and North America apart. When Columbus crossed the Atlantic in 1492, it was 20m narrower than it is today.

Columbus's flagship, the Santa Maria

Mid-Atlantic ridge

The longest mountain range in the world, the Mid-Atlantic Ridge, runs down the middle of the Atlantic Ocean. The mountains are up to 4km high, but their tips are still 2.5km under the surface of the sea.

The Mid-Atlantic Ridge is over 11,000km long.

INTERNET LINKS
To find links to Web sites about the Atlantic Ocean, its wildlife, and hurricanes go to **www.usborne-quicklinks.com**

Two South Atlantic islands are record-breakingly remote. Bouvet Island is the most isolated island. It is 1,600km away from Africa. The remotest inhabited island is Tristan da Cunha, 1,500km from Africa.

Hurricanes

Many hurricanes begin in the Atlantic. They form as warm air rises over the equator. This causes low pressure, which sucks the winds into a whirling cloud. In 1992, Hurricane Andrew hit Florida, making more than a million people homeless.

The spiralling winds of a hurricane, seen here, can reach speeds of over 200kph.

Wreckage caused by a hurricane.

Turtle tour

Atlantic green turtles leave their feeding grounds in Brazil and swim 2,000km to lay their eggs on Ascension Island in the middle of the Atlantic. Scientists believe they find their way with an in-built magnetic compass.

Atlantic green turtles swim halfway across the Atlantic to lay their eggs.

Spouting off

Waterspouts are common in the Gulf of Mexico. They form when tornadoes pass from land to sea. Winds blowing up to 965kph whip the sea into clouds of spray. Waterspouts can be 120m high.

A waterspout off the Florida coast

Still waters

The Sargasso Sea in the North Atlantic is an area of calm water larger than India. Huge rafts of seaweed float on its surface, sheltering some unique animals. The Sargassum fish is camouflaged to look like seaweed.

Can you see the Sargassum fish hiding in the seaweed?

Each year, eels swim from rivers in Europe to breed in the Sargasso Sea. The adults then die, and the young eels begin an amazing return journey. They are only 8cm long, but they swim 6,000km in about three years.

Young eel (half life size)

Lobster conga

Each year, thousands of spiny lobsters migrate over 100km along Florida's Atlantic coast. Troops of about 50 lobsters march in single file, as fast as a human can swim, hooking their claws round the lobster in front.

Spiny lobster

Unsalty sea

For 180km off the coast of Brazil, the Atlantic is hardly salty at all. This is due to the huge amount of water poured into it by the Amazon River. The Amazon carries over half the fresh water on earth.

The Indian Ocean

Vital statistics

Area	73,600,000km²
Widest part	10,000km
Average depth	3,900m
Greatest depth	9,000m
Volume	292,131,000km³

Warm 'n' salty

The Indian Ocean is the third largest ocean. It is also the warmest and saltiest. The surface temperature in the Persian Gulf can reach 35.6°C in summer. The Red Sea is the saltiest sea in the world*.

Persian Gulf
India
Red Sea
Africa
Indian Ocean

Flying fish

To escape enemies, flying fish shoot out of the water at speeds of over 30kph. They then glide over the surface using their tails as propellers and fins as wings. After about 40m, they bounce on the surface to give them extra lift. They can glide for up to 400m.

Flying fish can glide twice as fast as they swim.

Flying fish are found in the Indian Ocean.

Killer cone

The Indian Ocean is home to the most dangerous snail in the world: the cone shell. Inside its shell it has a trunk-like tube, full of deadly poison, which it injects into its prey.

Flying fish take off from the sea by rapidly flapping their tails.

At night, the surface of the Indian Ocean sparkles with light made by tiny plants called dinoflagellates**. Large numbers of them give off enough light to read by.

Cone shell feeding on a small cowrie

Pearly nautilus

The pearly nautilus lives in the Indian Ocean. Its shell is split into 40 chambers. It lives in the largest one. By altering the amount of gas in the chambers, the nautilus makes itself either float or sink.

Nautilus shell

* The Dead Sea is saltier, but is counted as a lake; **See *Red alert*, page 19

Coelacanth – not extinct after all.

Flashy fish

Many Indian Ocean fish have bright colours. This helps them to hide in the colourful reefs, and tells predators that they might be poisonous.

Blue moon angelfish

Golden butterfly fish

INTERNET LINKS
To find links to Indian Ocean Web sites, go to **www.usborne-quicklinks.com**

Deep sea fan

Sediment (mud and rocks) from the Indus and Ganges rivers pours into the Indian Ocean. It sinks to the bottom to form layers hundreds of metres thick. Undersea avalanches carry the sediment downwards, where it fans out, forming the "Bengal Fan". It stretches halfway across the Indian Ocean.

Alternating current

Most currents flow in one direction all the time. In the northern Indian Ocean, though, monsoon winds cause them to alter their direction twice a year. From October to April the currents are blown towards Africa. In May the currents flow towards India.

May-October: →
October-April: ⇒

Big bang

In 1883, a huge eruption blew up two thirds of the island of Krakatoa in the Indian Ocean. The sound was the loudest ever recorded. It was heard over 4,800km away in Australia.

The shockwaves caused a huge tsunami to sweep over Java and Sumatra. It killed 36,000 people, and carried boats 3km inland.

These are the remains of Krakatoa, which blew up in 1883.

A map showing the spread of the Bengal Fan in the Indian Ocean

This volcano is Anak Krakatau. It erupted from the sea in 1930.

The Arctic Ocean

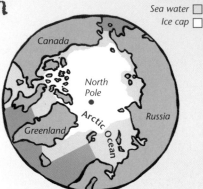

The Arctic Ocean is the smallest and shallowest ocean. It is almost entirely surrounded by land. It is frozen for most of the year, with the North Pole in the centre of a huge, floating raft of ice (the"ice cap"). In winter, the ice cap is up to 1.5km thick.

Vital statistics

Area	14,090,000km²
Area of ice	10,000,000km² (permanent)
	14,090,000km² (winter)
Sea ice* thickness	3m (average)
Average depth	1,300m
Greatest depth	5,450m

Iced water

Fresh water freezes at 0°C, but sea water at -2°C because salt lowers the freezing point. Frozen sea water, though, contains very little salt, as only the water part freezes. It can be melted down to make drinking water.

Sea unicorns

Male narwhals in the Arctic Ocean have a special feature shared by no other whale. They have a tusk which extends from their upper lips. It is actually a tooth, and can grow 2.5m long.

In the Middle Ages, narwhal tusks were sold as unicorn horns.

Polar bears can stand 1½ times the height of a person (2.6m).

Drifting off

The Arctic gets its name from the Greek word *arktos*, meaning "bear". It is home to huge polar bears, which can weigh over a tonne. Some bears drift for hundreds of kilometres out to sea on ice rafts. Some never go on land in their lives.

Polar bears are the largest type of bear, yet a newborn cub is so tiny that its mother can hide it between her toes. A cub grows so fast, though, that in a year it is as big as an adult human.

Polar bear cubs stay with their mothers for at least 2 years.

Sea ice: ice floating on the sea around the main ice cap

Midnight Sun

In June and July the North Pole has constant daylight. At the same time, the South Pole has 24 hour darkness. In December and January it is the South Pole's turn for the "midnight Sun" and the North Pole is freezing and dark.

Midsummer at the North Pole
The Earth's tilt gives the North Pole 24 hour sunshine.

Midwinter at the North Pole
The Earth's tilt keeps the North Pole in the dark.

Icebreakers

Icebreakers are ships used to break through thick sea ice. They have sloping bows which pull the ship up onto the ice ahead. The ship's weight then presses down and breaks a path through the ice.

An icebreaker moving through ice

Not all icebergs are white. They range in colour from pure white to blue, green or even black. The colour of icebergs is affected by their size, age and minerals in the ice.

Old icebergs are often blue.

Orca ahoy

Orcas, also called killer whales, are one of the Arctic Ocean's most fearsome predators, although they are not known to harm humans. They usually hunt in groups, and share their kills.

Orcas often hold their heads above the water to look around. This is called spy hopping.

Fire and ice

Deep under the Arctic Ocean is the Gakkel Ridge, a chain of volcanoes that runs for 1,500km. A rift running down the centre of the ridge contains vents*. Hot water gushing from the vents warms the ocean, and animals such as shrimp and sponges flourish there.

*See *Black smokers*, page 23

INTERNET LINKS
To find links to Web sites about the Arctic, and Arctic animals, go to
www.usborne-quicklinks.com

The Southern Ocean

The Southern Ocean is made up of the seas around Antarctica. In winter, an area of ocean twice the size of Canada is totally frozen over.

The Southern Ocean

Vital statistics

Area	35,000,000km²
Area of ice	4,000,000km² (permanent)
	21,000,000km² (in winter)
Sea ice thickness	0.75m (average)
Average depth	4,200m
Greatest depth	7,235m

Southern seals

The Weddell seal lives further south than any other mammal. It has to dive over 300m under the ice to find food. It can stay under for an hour, but must surface to breathe.

Weddell seals gnaw air holes in the ice with their big front teeth.

Millennium ocean

The boundary of the Southern Ocean was the last to be decided. In the year 2000, it was agreed worldwide that a circle of ocean ringing the continent of Antarctica would be known as the Southern Ocean. Its waters used to belong to the Atlantic, Pacific and Indian Oceans.

Round and round

The Southern Ocean flows clockwise around Antarctica. It is driven by the fast Antarctic circumpolar current. This is the largest of all currents, holding 100 times the water of all the world's rivers.

There are no penguins in the Arctic. They only live south of the equator. The four species found in Antarctica are well suited to the cold. Their feathers form windproof, waterproof coats so warm that the penguins can get too hot. They ruffle their feathers and extend their flippers to cool down.

Gentoo penguin

Some Antarctic cod have a chemical in their blood which acts as a natural antifreeze. It keeps their blood liquid even if the ocean temperature is several degrees below freezing.

Antarctic cod

Sky lights

In both the Arctic and the Antarctic, swirling light displays, called auroras, can be seen in the sky. They are caused by electrically charged particles in the atmosphere colliding with atoms of gas.

Ice mountains

The Southern and Arctic Oceans are littered with icebergs. These break off glaciers or ice sheets. The largest iceberg ever was seen off the Antarctic coast in 1956. Above water, its surface area was larger than Belgium.

Iced soup

Despite the cold, the Southern Ocean teems with life. In summer the water holds a huge amount of plankton which is eaten by small animals, such as krill. The krill are eaten in turn by birds, seals and whales. Krill form swarms so vast they can be seen from satellites.

Antarctic krill, half life-size

The aurora australis, also called the southern lights, glows above Antarctica.

INTERNET LINKS
To find links to Web sites about the Southern Ocean go to
www.usborne-quicklinks.com

The world's largest icebergs are found in the Southern Ocean.

41

Early Sea Explorers

From the 15th to the 18th centuries, many great explorers set out to discover new trade routes across the oceans. The map below shows some of the most famous voyages of that time.

- Christopher Columbus (1492-1493)
- Vasco da Gama (1497-1499)
- Ferdinand Magellan (1519-1522)
- Francis Drake (1577-1580)
- William Barents (1594-1596)
- James Cook (1768-1780)

The first sea expedition in history was made by a North African called Hanno in 2750 BC. He sailed down the Red Sea to explore the coast of Africa, later returning with spices and treasure.

Early traders hoped to find rare spices. This is pepper growing in the wild.

Viking voyagers

The Vikings may have been the first Europeans to reach America. In about 986, Eric the Red voyaged to Greenland, and started a settlement there. Later, his son, Leif the Lucky, is thought to have sailed across the Atlantic to America.

The Vikings sailed 600km across the Atlantic in ships like this.

Chris's miss

Columbus is famous for reaching America, but he only found it by accident. He sailed west from Spain, looking for a route to Asia. When he came to the Bahamas he thought he had found China. He never realized his mistake.

Studying the sea

HMS Challenger set out in 1872, from Portsmouth, England, on the first scientific voyage round the world. The expedition lasted for 3½ years, and its zig-zag route covered a distance of over 100,000km.

HMS Challenger's sealife laboratory

HMS Challenger was the first ship to sail all around the globe for science.

The achievements of HMS Challenger

- Measured the depth of the oceans, discovering, on the way, the deepest part of the Pacific, now named the Challenger Deep

- Discovered the Mid-Atlantic Ridge* – although many people at the time thought it was the fabled sunken continent of Atlantis

- Discovered over 4,000 new species of ocean animals and plants

- Discovered that life existed in the ocean's deepest, coldest depths

- The first in depth study of ocean currents and temperatures

Monstrous maps

Hundreds of years ago, sea travel was perilous as many seas were uncharted. People imagined that all kinds of terrifying creatures lived in the oceans. Old maps are often illustrated with these monsters.

Great ball of steel

In 1934, William Beebe and Otis Barton set an ocean depth record. They were lowered on a chain 923m into the ocean off Bermuda, in a large steel ball called a bathysphere. They reported what they saw through its tiny porthole, by telephone, back to those on the surface.

Beebe and Barton by their bathysphere in Bermuda

A map full of monsters

INTERNET LINKS
To find links to Web sites about early ocean explorers, and ocean scientists, go to **www.usborne-quicklinks.com**

*See page 34

Modern Exploration

Jacques Cousteau and Émile Gagnan invented scuba* gear in 1943. Scuba gear is made up of cylinders of compressed air, a mouthpiece, and a "regulator", which feeds the diver just the right amount of air.

Scuba gear allows divers to work at depths of up to 70m.

INTERNET LINKS
To find links to Web sites about exploring the ocean today go to **www.usborne-quicklinks.com**

Sea floor maps

Scientists map deep-sea features, such as ridges, using echoes. Scientific instruments are towed above the seabed to chart areas 60km wide. Satellites are used to map sea depth by looking for changes in the Earth's gravity.

Satellite map of part of the North Atlantic Ocean

Record breakers

In 1958, the American nuclear submarine *Nautilus* crossed the Arctic Ocean beneath the ice, a distance of 2,945km. It was the first vessel to reach the North Pole. In 1960, the nuclear submarine *Triton* made the first underwater trip around the world.

Deep divers

Atmospheric diving suits (ADS) have built-in air supplies. They let divers work safely hundreds of metres below the sea.

A "Wasp" ADS has metal hands agile enough to do a jigsaw puzzle.

! Divers sometimes suffer from "the bends". Nitrogen gas in their air supplies dissolves in the blood. If divers rise too quickly, nitrogen bubbles form in their blood. This can cause sharp pains, or even death.

Scuba is short for Self-Contained Underwater Breathing Apparatus.

Diving record	Greatest depth	Year set	Holder
Holding breath	152m	2000	Loic Leferme (France)
Scuba (breathing air)	155m	1994	Daniel Manion (USA)
Scuba (breathing gas mixture)	308m	2001	John Bennett (UK)
Helmeted dive	534m	1988	Operation Comex Hydra 8 (France)
Submersible	10,978m	1995	*Kaiko* (Japan)

Alvin

Submersibles are small submarines used for deep-sea exploration. The submersible *Alvin* has mechanical arms, which are used to collect seabed samples, such as mud and rocks.

Scientists in Alvin discovered deep sea vents* in the Pacific in 1977.

The crew are in a cabin only 2m wide.

Deep driller

A ship named the *JOIDES Resolution* has a huge drill that can bore into seabed 8,000m below. It removes cores (long cylinders) of rock. Studying the cores tells scientists how Earth's climate has changed during its history.

In 1960, the submersible *Trieste* dived 10,916m – almost to the bottom of the Pacific's Mariana Trench. It took 4hrs, 48 minutes. The crew were housed in a steel sphere with walls 13cm thick. This stopped them being crushed by the huge pressure.

The crew of the Trieste were in the steel sphere below the sub.

Robosub

AUVs (Automated Underwater Vehicles) are robot submarines. *Autosub*, an AUV operated by scientists in Southampton, England, can work in areas that are otherwise hard to reach, such as under the polar ice.

Autosub (yellow) is launched from a crane.

The drill ship JOIDES Resolution

*Deep-sea vents, see Black smokers, page 23

Ships and Shipwrecks

The first boats

The first boats were made by hollowing out tree trunks with fire or sharp tools. This is why they are called "dug-outs". The earliest known dug-out was found in Holland and is about 8,500 years old.

Sailing ships

The ancient Egyptians were the first people to use sails, 5,000 years ago. These first sails were square, and made of reeds.

The first sailing boats were used on the river Nile in Egypt.

The first submarine was invented in 1620 by Cornelius van Drebbel, a Dutch doctor. Its wooden frame was covered in greased leather, and it was rowed by 12 oars. Tubes to the surface provided air. It could travel at depths of 5m for several hours.

The Vasa

In 1628, the Swedish warship *Vasa* first set sail. Unfortunately, its many guns made it top-heavy, and minutes later it toppled and sank. A third of its crew drowned. In 1956, the *Vasa*'s wreck was found. It was later raised and preserved.

It took a thousand oak trees to build the Vasa.

Finding the way

For many years, sailors navigated by the Sun, Moon and stars. They used instruments called sextants to plot the ship's position by measuring the height of the Sun or Moon above the horizon at certain times of day.

A brass sextant

Sea speed

Speed at sea is measured in knots. One knot is one nautical mile (1.85km) per hour. To find a ship's speed, sailors in the past trailed a rope in the sea, knotted at even intervals. They counted the number of knots let out in 28 seconds.

INTERNET LINKS
To find links to Web sites about ships, shipwrecks and more go to
www.usborne-quicklinks.com

Famous shipwreck	Date sank	Items recovered
Kyrenia ship (Greece)	4th century BC	400 wine jars; 10,000 almonds
La Trinidad Valencera (Spain)	1588	Bronze cannons each weighing 2.5 tonnes
Vergulde Draeck (Holland)	1656	8 chests full of silver
Whydah (America)	1717	Pirate treasure worth £250 million
Geldermalsen (Holland)	1752	Rare china crockery; gold ingots
HMS Edinburgh (Great Britain)	1942	5.5 tonnes of gold bars, worth £45 million

The *RMS Titanic* was 260m long and weighed over 53,000 tonnes. It was the largest ship of its day. The links of its anchor chains were 90cm long, and each weighed 80kg. Its main anchor was 4m long, and weighed 16 tonnes.

Titanic discovery

In 1977, Robert Ballard, an ocean scientist, tried to find the *Titanic*'s wreck. His attempt failed when all his equipment was lost at sea. Joining others, he returned in 1985. After five weeks' search, the *Titanic* was found 640km off north-east Canada.

Raft journey

Thor Heyerdahl's Kon-tiki at sea

In 1947, the explorer Thor Heyerdahl set out in his balsa-wood raft, the *Kon-tiki*, to sail from Peru to the Pacific Islands. He wanted to prove that Inca people could have made the trip 1,500 years ago, and populated the islands. His crew reached the island of Raroia in under four months.

Iceberg ahoy!

Icebergs are a danger to ships because only about an eighth of the ice shows above the water. On the *Titanic*'s first voyage in 1912 she hit an iceberg in the north Atlantic and sank. Over 1,500 people died.

The bow of the Titanic, viewed from a deep sea submersible

Fewer than a third of the Titanic's passengers escaped to safety.

47

Sea Travel Today

Sea traffic

Over 90% of goods transported around the world go by sea. So that sea traffic may travel smoothly, there are certain shipping routes, ("lanes"), in the oceans that ships usually follow.

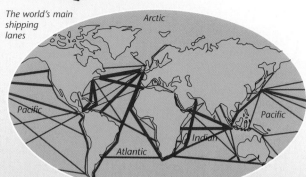

The world's main shipping lanes

Arctic

Pacific

Pacific

Atlantic

Indian

Southern

Parts of a ship

Port quarter   Port side   Port bow

Starboard quarter   Starboard side   Starboard bow

Astern   Aft   Forward   Ahead

Stern   HULL   Bow

Keel

Rudder

Enough shipping containers exist on the Earth to build a 5m high wall around the equator. Shipping containers are big metal boxes of a fixed size, mostly 6m or 12m long, used for carrying all kinds of cargo.

Shipping containers allow cargo to be loaded and unloaded quickly at ports.

Sea cats

Catamarans are boats with two hulls. This means less of the boat touches water, reducing friction so it can travel more quickly. *The Cat* is a catamaran ferry with a real cutting edge. Its sharp bows pierce the waves, letting it speed to 70kph.

The Cat runs between Maine, USA, and Nova Scotia, Canada.

BAY ferries

Buoys and marks

Ships stay safe by paying close attention to buoys, which are the roadsigns of the sea, and horn signals with special meanings:

Isolated danger mark

This buoy marks a dangerous area: avoid. Lights: two flashes

Safe water mark

This buoy marks a safe area. Lights: one long flash

Horn signals

One short blast:
Turning to starboard
Two short blasts:
Turning to port

Direction marks

Buoy	Direction of safe water	Lights (white)
	North	Continuous flashing
	East	Three quick flashes
	South	Six quick flashes + one long
	West	Nine quick flashes

INTERNET LINKS
To find links to Web sites about ships and shipping today, go to
www.usborne-quicklinks.com

Each year, lifeboats in the UK and Ireland alone save over 1,600 lives. All-weather class lifeboats are tough and totally watertight. If knocked over by fierce waves, they will bob upright almost immediately.

The UK and Ireland lifeboat services are run by volunteers.

Supertankers

The largest ships afloat are supertankers. They travel between the Middle East, Europe, America and Asia, each carrying enough oil to power a small city for a year. The *Jahre Viking* is the biggest: it is so long, its crew use bicycles to get around.

Stopping a supertanker is no easy task: it takes over 6km to bring the Jahre Viking to a halt.

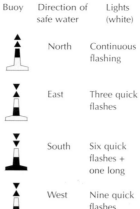

Vessel record	Name	Statistics
Largest vessel	ULCC* *Jahre Viking* (oil supertanker)	458m long; can carry 4.1 million oil barrels
Largest warship	USS *Harry S. Truman* (aircraft carrier)	334m long; flight deck 18,211m²
Largest cruise liner	*Voyager of the Seas*	310m long; can carry 3,114 passengers
Water speed	*Spirit of Australia* (hydroplane)	Reached a speed of 511kph (1978)
Largest sailing ship	*Royal Clipper*	42 sails, using 5,202m² of canvas

*ULCC: *Ultra Large Crude Carrier*

49

Ocean Resources

Sea harvest

Each year, some 90 million tonnes of fish are caught in the oceans. Over half comes from the Pacific. In 1986, a Norwegian boat took over 120 million fish in a single catch: enough for each Norwegian to have 26 each.

Most caught fish	Caught in 2000
Peruvian anchovy	11.3 million tonnes
Alaska pollock	3.0 million tonnes
Atlantic herring	2.3 million tonnes
Skipjack tuna	1.9 million tonnes
Japanese anchovy	1.7 million tonnes
Chilean jack mackerel	1.5 million tonnes

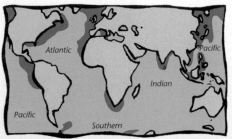

The pink areas on this map show the parts of the ocean where most of the world's fish are caught.

INTERNET LINKS
To find links to Web sites about the resources of the seas and oceans, go to **www.usborne-quicklinks.com**

Seaweed sandwich

Seaweed is full of vitamins and calcium. In China and Japan huge amounts are harvested and eaten. In Ireland it is spread over the fields as fertilizer. Seaweed is also used to thicken ice cream and to make shampoo, toothpaste and even explosives.

Seaweed... yum!

Gold mine

Sea water contains about 400 times more gold than is owned on land. Sea gold has already been mined on the coasts of Alaska. If all the sea gold was mined, there would be enough for everyone on Earth to have a piece weighing over 4kg.

Fish farming

Many countries breed fish in undersea farms. On fish farms, plaice grow to full size in 18-24 months: half the time it takes in the wild. They are also easier to catch than in the open sea.

A Norwegian salmon farm

About 66 million tonnes of salt are taken from the sea each year. In hot countries, it is done by drying sea water in huge pans left in the Sun.

The sea salt produced in a year would make a pile nearly three times as high as Egypt's Great Pyramid.

Ocean oil

Over a fifth of the world's oil comes from the seabed. Oil formed millions of years ago from the bodies of tiny sea animals and plants which drifted to the sea bed and were covered in layers of mud and sand.

Offshore oil producers	Barrels produced daily
Norway	3,230,000
Mexico	2,500,000
UK	2,180,000
Saudi Arabia	1,990,000
United Arab Emirates	1,150,000
USA	1,060,000

Taming the tides

Scientists are now looking to the sea as a source of energy. The world's first tidal power station was built on the River Rance in France. A dam with 24 tunnels in it runs across the river mouth. As the tides rush in and out, they turn generators in the tunnels which produce electricity.

Some scientists think that Antarctic icebergs could provide desert areas with fresh water. Boats could tow large icebergs to Africa, for example. Wrapping the icebergs in plastic could contain the ice that melts.

Icebergs – the answer to drought in hot countries?

Deep sea nodules

A quarter of the Pacific Ocean floor is covered in black, potato-sized lumps, or nodules. These contain valuable metals, such as nickel and manganese. Over millions of years the nodules grow in layers around small objects, such as grains of sand or even sharks' teeth.

Black lumps like these litter the ocean floor.

Each of the 24 generators at the Rance tidal power station makes enough power to light a medium-sized town.

Cormorant droppings are used as fertilizer.

Priceless poo

Sea bird droppings, or guano, are the world's most valuable natural fertilizer – 30 times richer than farmyard manure. For thousands of years, millions of cormorants have nested on Peru's cliffs. At times, parts of the cliffs were covered in a layer of guano 50m thick.

Oceans in Danger

Over 80% of the waste polluting the oceans comes from the land. Here are some of the main causes of pollution:

- Sewage pumped into the sea
- Nuclear waste from power plants
- Poisonous metals, such as mercury, tin and lead, from factories, mines and boats
- Chemical fertilizers and pesticides, washed off farmland and carried by rivers to the sea.
- Oil and petrol are washed off the land into the sea. Oil also comes from oil rig and tanker accidents.

Oil ruins seabirds' feathers, and they die of cold.

A striped dolphin caught in a drift net

Sick slick

In March 1989, the oil tanker, *Exxon Valdez*, ran aground in Prince William Sound, Alaska. In one of the worst oil spills ever, 45 million litres of oil poured into the sea, killing hundreds of thousands of sea birds and animals.

The Exxon Valdez oilspill

Plastic drift nets are trailed across the ocean like giant walls: just one net may be 20km long. Each year, thousands of sea mammals and birds die when they become entangled in drift nets used for catching squid.

Fight to survive

The Mediterranean monk seal is Europe's most endangered mammal. They have been killed for their meat and skins, and by fishermen who see them as pests.

Fewer than 400 Mediterranean monk seals remain

Plenty more fish in the sea?

Fish are being taken from the world's oceans faster than they can breed. This is called overfishing. Off Canada's east coast, for example, fishing Atlantic cod is banned, as very few remain.

In some countries, nets with a large mesh are used to let young fish escape.

INTERNET LINKS
To find links to Web sites about the dangers threatening the oceans, go to
www.usborne-quicklinks.com

Suffocated sea

In summer, seas polluted with waste fertilizer and sewage may be covered in a thick, green slime of phytoplankton*. The plankton uses minerals in the waste to grow. It blocks out sunlight other sea plants need. As it rots, it uses up so much oxygen that many sea creatures suffocate.

Phytoplankton comes in many shapes and sizes.

Endangered sea animals	Population	Major threats
Blue whale	Under 4,000	Pollution; some hunting
Fin whale	50–100,000	Pollution
Kemp's Ridley turtle	Under 4,000	Shrimp fishing nets
Florida manatee	Under 3,500	Killed by motor boats
Juan Fernandez fur seal	About 12,000	Hunting
Sea otter	Under 2,500	Hunting; oil pollution

Marine park

The Great Barrier Reef is home to 400 species of coral and 1,500 species of fish. In 1980, the Barrier Reef Marine Park was set up to protect the reef from tourists, pollution and overfishing. There are now special areas set aside for nesting sites, research, fishing and tourists.

Law of the sea

The Law of the Sea aims to protect the sea and control how it is used. It was drawn up by the United Nations in 1982. It divides the sea up into areas for different countries, leaving about two thirds of the open ocean free for all.

The name "penguin" was first given to a now-extinct North Atlantic bird, later called the great auk. What we call penguins were named after these birds because they looked like them.

Scientists believe that, unless action is taken to save them, more than half of the world's coral reefs could be destroyed by 2030.

The great auk could not fly, so it was easy to hunt. The last one was killed in 1844.

*See page 18

The Future of the Sea

Able cable

The Internet's future lies in the world's longest undersea fibre-optic telecoms cable. Called *Sea-Me-We 3*, it runs for 39,000km, and connects countries from Germany to Japan and Australia. It can carry the equivalent of 4,000 encyclopedias' worth of information in a second.

Water power

Ocean Thermal Energy Conversion (OTEC) makes energy from tropical seas. Warm surface water is pumped into a special ship, where it warms tanks of an easy-boiling liquid. The gas produced drives turbines, making electricity. Cold water is then pumped in to cool the gas back to liquid, and the process restarts.

Cold water pumped in here

OTEC ships could make energy if oil and gas reserves ever run low.

Deep Flight

If built, the futuristic Deep Flight II will take explorers to the deepest parts of the ocean.

Submersibles must lose or gain weight to rise and sink. This limits their speed. Graham Hawkes*, a leading inventor of manned submersibles, is building speedy "Deep Flight" subs that stay the same weight, but fly like planes.

Deep Flight subs have stubby, upside-down wings for speeding down into the depths of the sea.

A ship up-ended is usually bad news, but scientists in the USA have a ship that flips on purpose. *R/V FLIP* flips and floats upright, cutting out wave noise so its crew can study undersea sounds. When it flips, the crew walk on its walls! Longer "flip ships" may one day be built to work in deeper seas.

Don't worry – it's meant to do this

Farming the seas

Overfishing (see page 52) is seriously reducing the world's fish population. Fish farming, already common in places such as Norway, could help numbers grow again. In the future, more fish may be farmed than are caught in the wild.

 *Turn to page 44 to see Graham Hawkes in the Wasp, a diving suit he designed.

INTERNET LINKS
To find links to Web sites about the future
of the oceans, and living under the sea,
go to **www.usborne-quicklinks.com**

Living underwater

Aquarius is an undersea
laboratory off the coast
of Florida, USA. It lets
scientists live and work
in the ocean without
having to keep returning
to a ship on the surface.
We may not see huge
undersea cities in the
future, but there may
well be more labs – and
even holiday resorts!

Robolobster!

In the future, robots modelled on sea
creatures may save lives. A robot
lobster, built in the USA, may be the
first of an army of robots which scuttle
over the seafloor, sniffing out deadly
mines with electronic feelers.

This robot
lobster can
walk in any
direction, just
like a real
lobster.

*Inside Aquarius, the world's only
undersea research laboratory.*

Medicines that may
help to fight cancer
have been made from
substances found in
coral, sponges and
other sealife. If we are
careful to protect the
world's sealife, we may
yet discover new cures
to many diseases.

*Corals have proved to contain
cancer-fighting chemicals.*

Floating city

Plans to build the largest cruise liner ever are
now underway. Called the *Freedom Ship*, it
will be 1.3km long, 25 storeys high, and house
50,000 people. It will be more like a city than
a cruise liner, with shops, schools, parks,
cafés, and its own airstrip. Unlike
any city, though, it will circle
the world once every
two years.

*If built, the Freedom
Ship will be the
biggest ship
ever.*

Sea Myths and Legends

The kraken

Norse legends tell of a huge sea monster, the kraken, which could turn a ship over. It was a cross between an octopus and a squid, with suckers, claws, and a beak strong enough to bore through wood.

The kraken legend may well be based on a giant squid.

Lost continent

The continent of Atlantis is said to have flourished in about 10,000 BC. It was then destroyed in a volcanic eruption, and sank without trace. No one knows if Atlantis really existed, but there are many theories about its location. These include the Greek island of Santorini, an island near Gibraltar, Cuba and Antarctica.

Ghost ship

The *Flying Dutchman* is said to bring bad luck to all who see her. The ship left Amsterdam for the East Indies in the 17th century. On the way back, she met a fierce storm. Her arrogant captain swore to the devil that he would sail through the storm, even if he had to sail until Judgement Day. His ship never returned. It is said that the ship was doomed to haunt the seas forever.

The Flying Dutchman was sighted during World War II by German submariners.

"Crossing the line" is an old custom on ships passing the equator. Those on board who have not crossed before ("pollywogs") are called before King Neptune and his court, played by the crew, who punish them for their "crimes", often by shaving and soaking them. They are then called "shellbacks".

King Neptune's sceptre is a three-pronged spear called a trident.

Abandoned ship

In 1872, a ship called the *Mary Celeste* was found drifting in the Atlantic. The whole crew had vanished, apparently in a hurry, leaving their boots. The lifeboats were also missing, but, to this day, no one knows for sure what happened to them.

INTERNET LINKS
To find links to Web sites about ocean myths and legends go to **www.usborne-quicklinks.com**

Dolphin rescue

A Greek legend tells how dolphins saved the life of the musician, Arion. He was sailing back to Greece after winning a music competition in Italy. The ship's crew wanted his prizes, and attacked him. They allowed him to play one last tune, which attracted a school of dolphins. Arion leapt overboard and was safely carried home on the dolphins' backs.

Ocean gods	Worshippers
Poseidon	Greeks
Neptune	Romans
Njörd	Norse
T'ien Hou (goddess of sailors)	Chinese
O-Wata-Tsu-Mi	Japanese
Tangaroa	Polynesians
Sedna	Inuit
Manannán mac Lir	Celts

Pictures of dolphins, like these, were often painted on ancient Greek pottery.

In ancient Greece, dolphins were sacred to the god Apollo, and it was illegal to harm them.

Very like a whale?

In 1852, two whaling ships, the *Monongahela* and the *Rebecca Sims*, harpooned what they thought was a whale, 4,000km west of Ecuador. When they hauled it in, they were amazed. It seemed to be a brownish-grey reptile, 45m long, with huge jaws full of sharp, curving teeth. The body was too huge to keep, so they cut off its head and preserved it in salt. The ships then headed home, but only the *Rebecca Sims* made it: the *Monongahela*, and the monster's head, were never seen again.

Clam creation

In Polynesian myth, the world was created in a giant clam. A goddess, Old Spider, squeezed inside a giant clam and found two snails and a worm. She made the smaller snail the Moon, and the larger one the Sun. Half the clam shell became the Earth, the other half the sky, and the worm's salty sweat became the sea.

Do sea serpents really exist?

57

Ocean Records

The oceans that cover two-thirds of our planet are full of record-breaking features and creatures. This map shows some of them.

Arctic Ocean
Smallest ocean:
14,090,000km^2

Longest undersea telecoms cable
Sea-Me-We 3
cable network:
39,000km

Hottest surface sea water
Persian Gulf:
35.6°C in
summer

Saltiest sea water
Red Sea
(4.2% salt)

Deepest point on Earth
Challenger
Deep, Mariana
Trench: 11,022m

Indian Ocean

Smallest sea fish
Dwarf goby: max.
length 8.9mm

Atlantic Ocean

Largest seabird
Wandering albatross:
3.5m wingspan

Longest coral reef:
Great Barrier Reef:
2,028km

Key to seas

1. South China Sea
2. Mediterranean Sea
3. Arabian Sea
4. Weddell Sea
5. Bering Sea
6. Caribbean Sea
7. Gulf of Mexico
8. Sea of Okhotsk
9. Sea of Japan
10. North Sea
11. Black Sea
12. Sargasso Sea

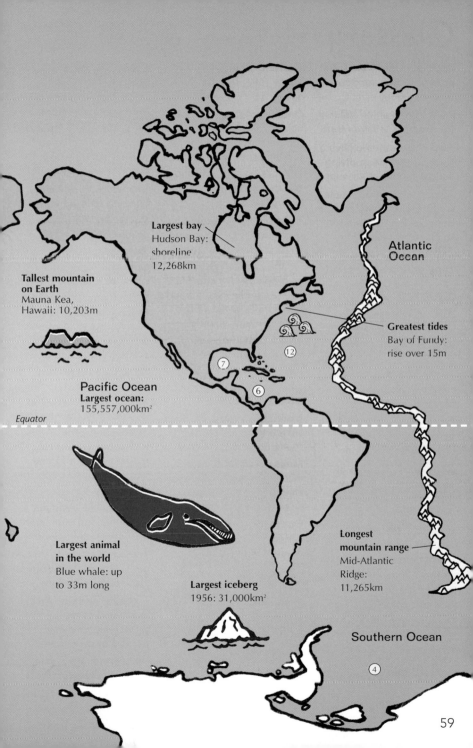

Largest bay
Hudson Bay:
shoreline
12,268km

Atlantic
Ocean

**Tallest mountain
on Earth**
Mauna Kea,
Hawaii: 10,203m

Greatest tides
Bay of Fundy:
rise over 15m

⑦

⑫

⑥

Pacific Ocean
Largest ocean:
155,557,000km²

Equator

**Largest animal
in the world**
Blue whale: up
to 33m long

**Longest
mountain range**
Mid-Atlantic
Ridge:
11,265km

Largest iceberg
1956: 31,000km²

Southern Ocean

④

Glossary

Abyssal plain A vast, flat area of the ocean floor, below 4,000m.

ACV Air Cushion Vehicle; for example, a hovercraft.

ADS Atmospheric Diving Suit: a hard, deep-diving suit with built-in air supply.

Algae A group of simple water plants, ranging from tiny, one-celled plankton to giant seaweed.

Atoll A circular, or horseshoe-shaped, coral island around a shallow lagoon.

AUV Autonomous Underwater Vehicle: a robot submersible.

Barnacle A small, shelled crustacean that sticks tightly to undersea objects and animals.

Bathysphere A metal sphere used in early deep sea exploration.

Cetaceans A group of sea mammals with no rear limbs, including whales and dolphins.

Continental shelf The shallow seabed around the continents, usually no deeper than 200m below sea level.

Continental slope The sloping area leading from the continental shelf to the abyssal plain.

Crustaceans A group of animals with hard shells and jointed legs, such as lobsters and shrimp.

Current A huge band of water running through the sea.

Dinoflagellates Tiny, one-celled sea plants. Some are poisonous; others produce their own light.

DSV Deep Submergence Vehicle: a deep sea submersible.

Equator An imaginary line dividing the northern and southern halves of the Earth.

Hydroplane A motorboat with an underside shaped to lift its bow out of the water at high speeds.

Invertebrate An animal without a backbone.

Knot A measurement of speed at sea. One knot equals 1.85kph.

Mammal A warm-blooded vertebrate with hair that feeds its young on milk.

Molluscs A large group of invertebrates, often with shells, ranging from limpets to giant squid.

Oceanography The scientific study of the oceans and seas.

Phytoplankton Tiny, drifting sea plants.

Pinnipeds A group of sea mammals including seals, sealions and walruses.

Plankton Tiny sea plants and animals which drift near the sea's surface.

Plate A piece of the Earth's hard crust.

Polyp A small sea invertebrate. Coral is made from millions of hard polyp skeletons.

ROV Remotely Operated Vehicle: an undersea vehicle operated from, and tethered to, a ship.

Seamount A volcano beneath the sea surface.

Seaquake An undersea earthquake.

Sediment Pieces of mud, sand and rock which settle on the seabed.

Siphonophore A jellyfish-like animal, such as a Portuguese man-of-war, which is made up of a colony of tiny animals.

Spreading ridge An undersea mountain range, formed when lava rises to fill cracks in the sea floor.

Subduction zone A place where two undersea plates collide and one plate is pushed under the other.

Submersible A small, freely-moving submarine used by ocean scientists.

Trench A deep, V-shaped dip in the seabed, formed at a subduction zone.

Turbidity current An avalanche of mud and sand, which may be caused by a seaquake.

Vertebrate An animal with a backbone.

Zooplankton Tiny, drifting sea animals.

Using the Internet

Internet links

Most of the Web sites described in this book can be accessed with a standard home computer and an Internet browser (the software that enables you to display information from the Internet). We recommend:

• A PC with Microsoft® Windows 98 or later version, or a Macintosh computer with System 9.0 or later, and 64Mb RAM
• A browser such as Microsoft® Internet Explorer 5, or Netscape® 6, or later versions
• Connection to the Internet via a modem (preferably 56Kbps) or a faster digital or cable line
• An account with an Internet Service Provider (ISP)
• A sound card to hear sound files

Extras

Some Web sites need additional free programs, called plug-ins, to play sounds, or to show videos, animations or 3-D images. If you go to a site and you do not have the necessary plug-in, a message saying so will come up on the screen. There is usually a button on the site that you can click on to download the plug-in. Alternatively, go to www.usborne-quicklinks.com and click on "Net Help". There you can find links to download plug-ins. Here is a list of plug-ins you might need:

RealPlayer® – lets you play videos and hear sound files
QuickTime – lets you view video clips
Shockwave® – lets you play animations and interactive programs
Flash™ – lets you play animations

Help

For general help and advice on using the Internet, go to **Usborne Quicklinks** at **www.usborne-quicklinks.com** and click on **Net Help**. To find out more about how to use your Web browser, click on **Help** at the top of the browser, and then choose Contents and Index. You'll find a huge searchable dictionary containing tips on how to find your way around the Internet.

Internet safety

Remember to follow the Internet safety guidelines at the front of this book. For more safety information, go to **Usborne Quicklinks** and click on **Net Help**.

Computer viruses

A computer virus is a program that can seriously damage your computer. A virus can get into your computer when you download programs from the Internet, or in an attachment (an extra file) that arrives with an e-mail. We strongly recommend that you buy anti-virus software to protect your computer, and that you update the software regularly.

INTERNET LINK
To find a link to a Web site where you can find out more about computer viruses, go to **www.usborne-quicklinks.com** and click on **Net Help**.

Index

Acknowledgements

Every effort has been made to trace the copyright holders of the material in this book. If any rights have been omitted, the publishers offer to rectify this in any subsequent editions following notification. The publishers are grateful to the following organizations and individuals for their permission to reproduce material (t=top, m=middle, b=bottom, l=left, r=right):

AP Photo/Michel Lipchitz: **47mr**
Bay Ferries: **48b**
Corbis: **10ml** Ralph A. Clevenger/CORBIS; **15l** Wolfgang Kaeler/CORBIS; **19tr** Douglas P. Wilson, Frank Lane Picture Agency/CORBIS; **23tl** Ralph White/CORBIS; **25m** Jeffrey L. Rottman/CORBIS; **28ml** Richard Cummins/CORBIS; **29b** Stephen Frink/CORBIS; **32-33 main** Nik Wheeler/CORBIS; **36m** Tony Arruza/CORBIS; **37b** Charles O'Rear/CORBIS; **38br** Dan Guravich/CORBIS; **39ml** Winifred Wisniewski, Frank Lane Picture Agency/CORBIS; **43mr** Ralph White/CORBIS; **47m** Ralph White/CORBIS; **48mr** Wolfgang Kaehler/CORBIS; **50mr** Paul A. Souders/CORBIS; **51ml** Yann Arthus-Bertrand/CORBIS; **br** Academy of Natural Sciences of Philadelphia/CORBIS; **53bl** Academy of Natural Sciences of Philadelphia/CORBIS
Courtesy of the Naval Historical Centre: **45mr**
Dr David Billett, Southampton Oceanography Centre: **22bl**
Digital Vision: **Title page; Half-title; 6mr; 7; 8-9; 13; 14m; 16-17b; 27mr; 28bl; 30m; 33tr; 34bl; br; bl; 40br; 40-41 main; 51tr; 52tr; 53br**
Dirk H.R. Spennemann, Albury NSW, Australia: **32br**
Freedom Ship International Inc.: **55b**
Getty Images: **28t** Stuart Westmorland
Prof. Gwyn Griffiths, Southampton Oceanography Centre: **45br**
Hawkes Ocean Technologies: **54m**
INCAT, Australia: **48b**
Jahre Dahl Bergesen: **49m**
Jan Witting, Northeastern University, Massachussets: **55tr**
Jeffrey Jeffords (**Divegallery.com**): **17r; 18b; 19r; 32m; 35br**
National Oceanic and Atmospheric Administration (NOAA)/Dept of Commerce: **12bl; 16ml; 19ml; 23r; bl; 25tl; 28mr; 35tr; ml; 36bl; 39mr; 41m; 43t; m; 44br; 51mr; 55ml**
NOAA/National Geophysical Data Centre: **44bl**
National Ocean Service (NOS) Photo Gallery: **14bl** Laura Francis/NOS; **24bl** Daniel Gotshall/NOS; **52m**
Ocean Drilling Program/Texas A&M University: **45bl**
Prof. Paul Tyler, Southampton Oceanography Centre/Prof. Craig Young, Harbor Branch Oceanographic Institute, Fort Pierce, Florida: **21b; mr**
RNLI/Robert Townsend: **49tr**
Science Photo Library: **11br** Astrid & Hanns-Frieder Michler/Science Photo Library
Scripps Institution of Oceanography: **54bm**
Sea Solar Power International: illustration on **54tr** based on their SSP 100 MW plantship
Stockbyte: **16-17b; 55mr**
Vasa Museum, Stockholm, Sweden: **46m**

Additional illustrators Mike Barber, Trevor Boyer, Peter Dennis, John Francis, Nigel Frey, Jeremy Gower, David Hancock, Alan Harris, Phillip Hood, Christine Howes, Ian Jackson, Chris Lyon, Malcolm McGregor, David Quinn, Michael Roffe, Chris Shields, Karen Tomlins

Usborne Publishing is not responsible and does not accept liability for the availability or content of any Web site other than its own, or for any exposure to harmful, offensive, or inaccurate material which may appear on the Web. Usborne Publishing will have no liability for any damage or loss caused by viruses that may be downloaded as a result of browsing the sites it recommends.

Material in this book is based on *The Usborne Book of Ocean Facts and Lists* by Anita Ganeri, © Usborne Publishing, 1990.